To my first great-granddaughter, Zion McKenzie Noel
and to all things that squeal, purr, roar, hoot, screech,
bark, meow, chirp, and neigh. —J. P.

JERRY PINKNEY

THE LION &
THE MOUSE

LITTLE, BROWN AND COMPANY
Books for Young Readers
New York   Boston

WHO

Who whoOoo

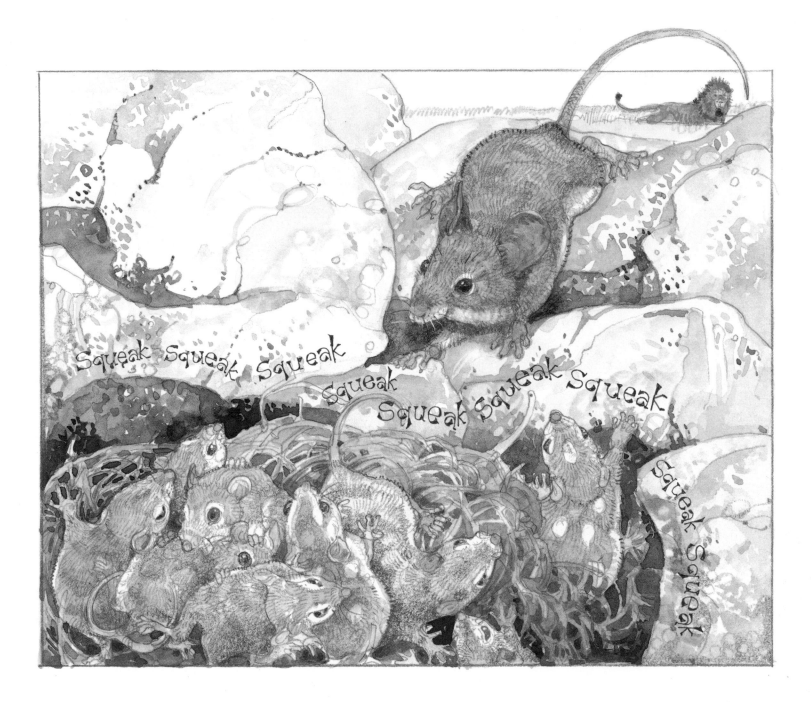

Putt-
Putt-
Putt

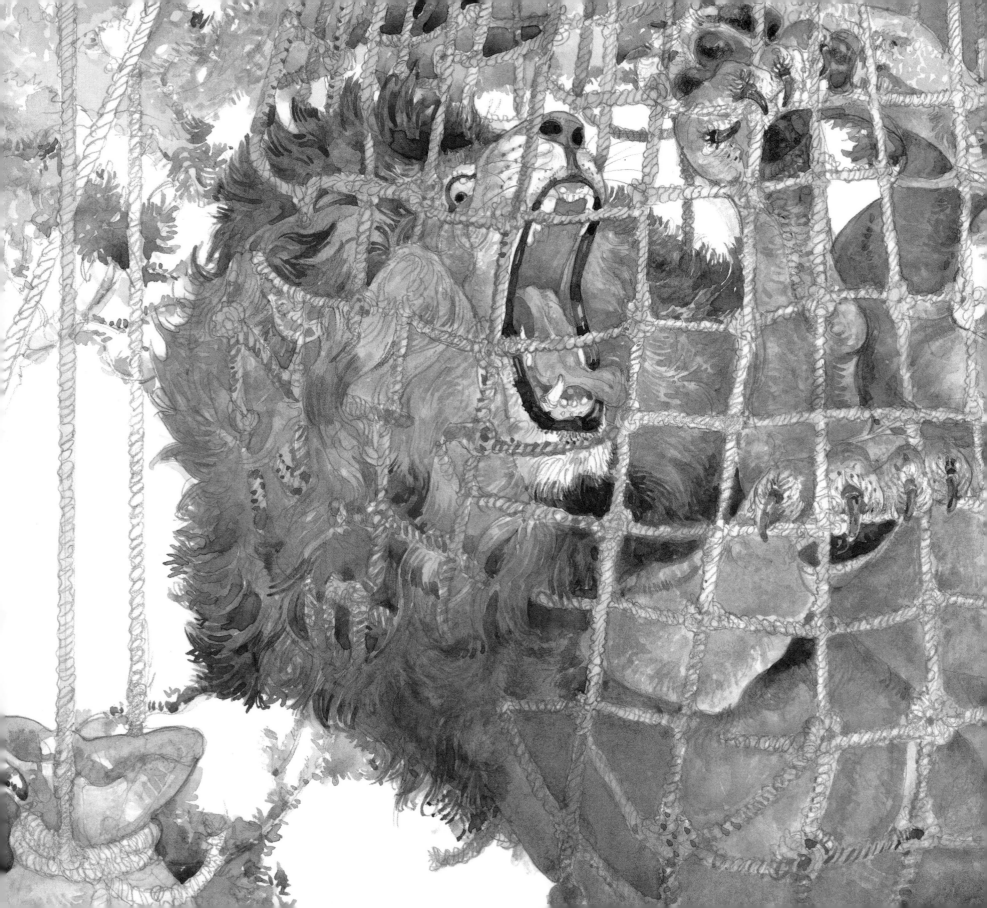

R R R R R R R R r r

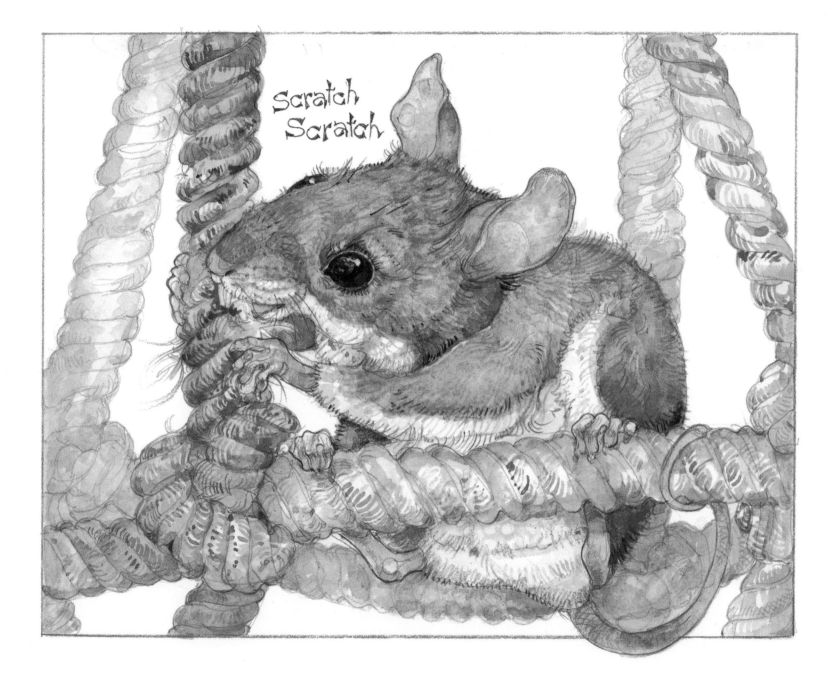

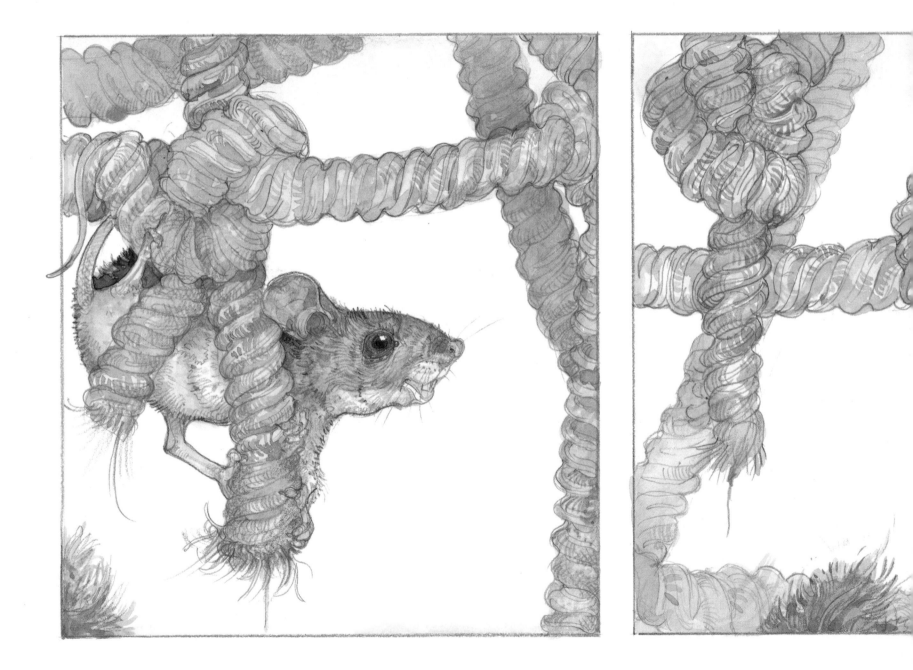

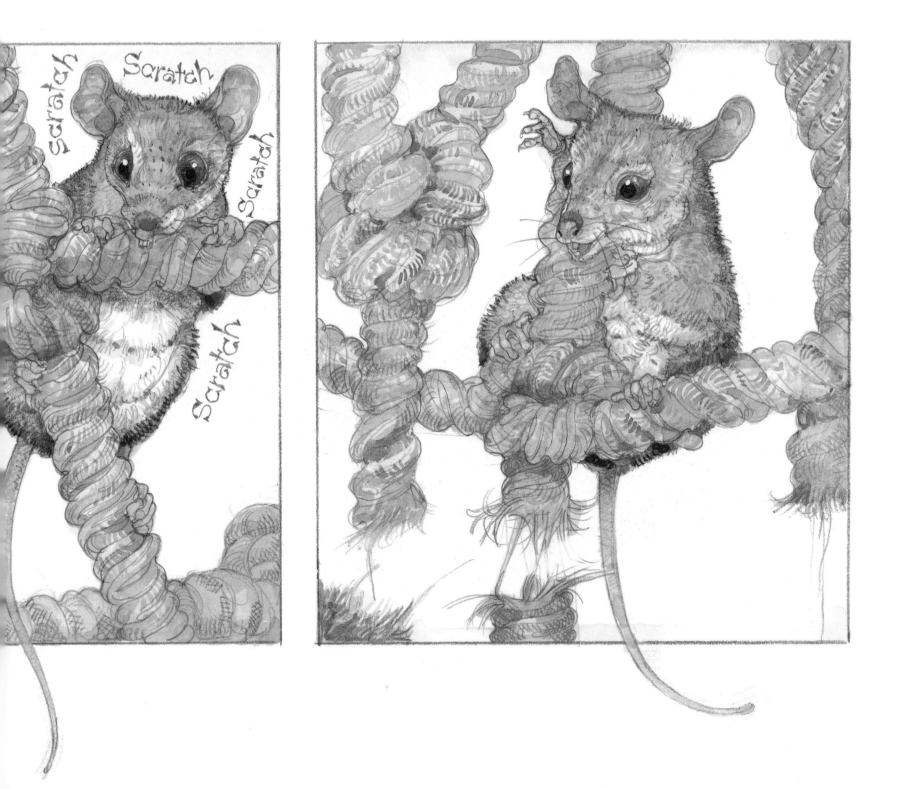

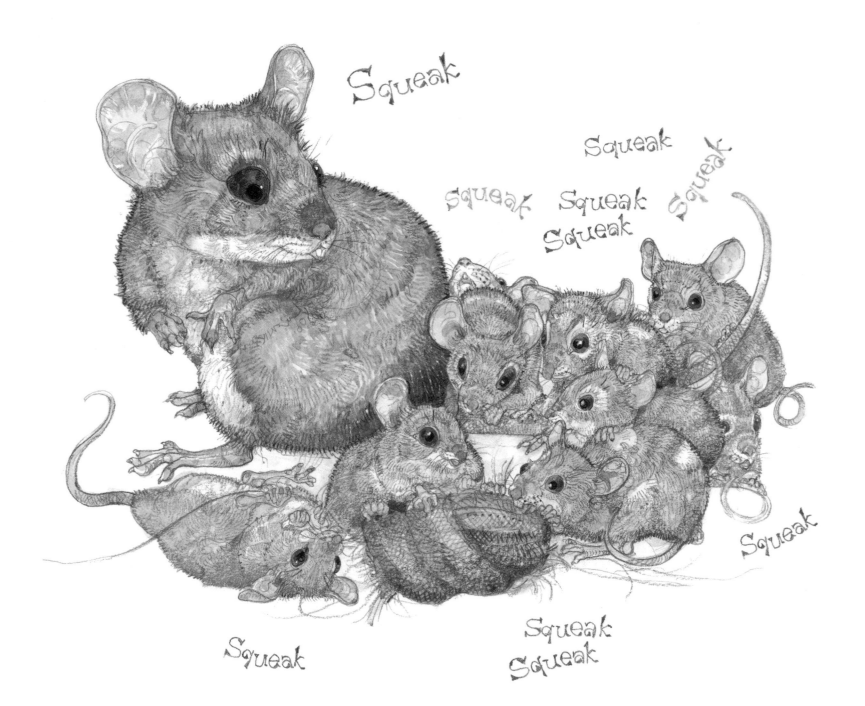

ARTIST'S NOTE

Of all Aesop's fables, "The Lion and the Mouse" is one of my childhood favorites: the tale of a mouse who accidentally disturbs a lion from his rest, and the lion who makes a life-changing decision to release his prey. When the mouse remembers her debt, she frees the lion from a poacher's trap. For me, this story offers far more than a simple moral of how the meek can trump the mighty.

Since working on my collection *Aesop's Fables*, I have felt drawn back to these two seemingly opposite characters. As a child I was inspired to see the majestic king of the jungle saved by the determination and hard work of a humble rodent; as an adult I've come to appreciate how both animals are *equally* large at heart: the courageous mouse, and the lion who must rise above his beastly nature to set his small prey free. It was gratifying, then, to place these two spirited creatures head-to-head on this book's jacket, each commanding powerful space and presence.

Since most retellings of the classic are sparse in text, a wordless version seemed quite natural; yet these engaging characters led me to make the story even fuller by providing a sense of family and setting. Living next to a nature preserve, I am fascinated with the vast medley of sounds coming from the surrounding woods, and that chorus of chatters and squeals helped shape the idea of selectively using animal sounds to gently enhance the story, while allowing the visuals—as well as the reader's imagination—to drive the narrative.

My curiosity and reverence for animal life has grown over the years, and my concern for them grows in equal measure. It seemed fitting, then, to stage this fable in the African Serengeti of Tanzania and Kenya, with its wide horizon and abundant wildlife so awesome yet fragile—not unlike the two sides of each of the heroes starring in this great tale for all times.

Jerry Pinkney

Text and illustrations copyright © 2009 by Jerry Pinkney • All rights reserved. Except as permitted under the U.S. Copyright Act of 1976, no part of this publication may be reproduced, distributed, or transmitted in any form or by any means, or stored in a database or retrieval system, without the prior written permission of the publisher. • Little, Brown Books for Young Readers • Hachette Book Group • 237 Park Avenue, New York, NY 10017 • Visit our Web site at www.lb-kids.com • Little, Brown Books for Young Readers is a division of Hachette Book Group, Inc. • The Little, Brown name and logo are trademarks of Hachette Book Group, Inc. • First Edition: September 2009 • Library of Congress Cataloging-in-Publication Data • Pinkney, Jerry. • The lion & the mouse / Jerry Pinkney. —1st ed. • p. cm. • Summary: In this wordless retelling of an Aesop fable, an adventuresome mouse proves that even small creatures are capable of great deeds when she rescues the King of the Jungle. • ISBN 978-0-316-01356-7 • [1. Fables. 2. Folklore. 3. Stories without words.] I. Aesop. II. Title. III. Title: Lion and the mouse. • PZ8.2.P456Li 2009 • 398.2—dc22 • [E] • 2008043852 • 10 9 8 7 6 5 • IM • Printed in Singapore • The full-color artwork for this book has been prepared using pencil, watercolor, and colored pencils on paper. • The text was set in Old Claude LP, and the display type was hand-lettered. • Design by Saho Fujii • Production by Adrienne Davis